THE
FABULOUS

The Very
Big
Secret

4

Enid Blyton

THE
FABULOUS

The Very
Big
Secret
4

Adapted and Edited by
Jenny Cooke

HarperCollins*Publishers*

HarperCollins*Publishers*
77–85 Fulham Palace Road, London W6 8JB
www.**fireandwater**.com

First published in Great Britain in 1952
by Lutterworth Press

This edited and adapted edition published in 2000
by HarperCollins*Publishers*

1 3 5 7 9 10 8 6 4 2

Copyright © 2000 Enid Blyton Ltd
Enid Blyton's signature is a trademark of Enid Blyton Ltd

A catalogue record for this book is
available from the British Library

ISBN 0 00 274085 0

Printed and bound in Great Britain by
Omnia Books Limited, Glasgow

Contents

1

At Corner Cottage

Everyone liked Corner Cottage. It had snow-drops and daffodils in the front garden in the spring, and roses all over the house in the summer. And each year the tall hollyhocks grew higher than the children who lived there.

A brother and sister lived at Corner Cottage. The boy was called Sam and the girl was called Rosie. Their father was a sailor and he was often away on his big ship. Their mother was a very nice mother indeed.

Corner Cottage was very small. There wasn't even room for a nursery or a playroom for the children, so Daddy had told the builder to put up a little playroom at the bottom of the garden for them.

'It's nice to have a playroom of our very,

very own,' Rosie often said to Sam. 'We're all by ourselves here and we can sing and whistle and make a noise, and nobody minds!'

'And I can have my railway lines all over the floor and I don't have to take them up till I want to,' said Sam. 'And we can build what we like and not have to clear up the bricks each night.'

'But I do wish John and Sarah were here to play with us,' said Rosie. John and Sarah were their cousins and they lived across the road at Whitewalls Cottage.

'Yes,' said Sam. 'What a shame they've gone on holiday at the moment.'

Mummy sometimes came down to have a look at the playroom, just to see if it was clean and fairly tidy. The children had to sweep and dust it every day and Mrs Mills, who came to help in the kitchen, turned the playroom out once a month. How the children hated that!

'I like keeping the playroom clean and tidy,' said Rosie each day, as she dusted the room carefully. 'I like putting flowers in our little vase. Do you like cleaning the windows, Sam?'

'Yes, quite,' said Sam. 'So long as you don't ask me to do it when I'm playing with my trains.'

The children had half of the playroom each for their toys. Sam had drawn a line across the floor to show where his half began and where Rosie's half ended. He had to keep his trains and boats and games strictly in his half, and Rosie kept her toys in hers. But if they wanted to play trains together, or build with the bricks, then they used the whole room.

You should have seen Rosie's half of the playroom. It seemed to be all dolls, dolls, dolls! Big dolls, little dolls, tiny dolls, rather grown-up dolls, toddler dolls and baby dolls; new dolls, old dolls and a dirty rag doll that Rosie had been given when she was a baby and still loved now.

One doll, Belinda, was very big indeed, as big as a real baby. Daddy had brought it back from America for Rosie. 'Look,' he said, 'this doll can open and shut her eyes. She can stand beautifully, and watch, Rosie, if you press this button here in her back, she cries!'

Rosie pressed the button. 'Oooh ... ow ...

3

ow … ow!' cried Belinda. 'Oooh … ow … ow … ow!'

'Oh! She sounds like a real baby,' said Rosie, startled, and she picked up Belinda and hugged her. 'Don't cry, Baby, don't cry!'

Belinda was Rosie's favourite. She was a real armful to hold. Mummy gave Rosie some of their old baby clothes to dress her in. She even gave Rosie the old plastic bath which she and Sam had been bathed in when they were tiny.

Sam liked that. The bath rested on a folding stand, and when it was unfolded and stood on its legs, Sam saw there was a little tap underneath the bath. He screwed it and unscrewed it.

'Look, Rosie,' he said, 'you screw this tap tight when the bath is full of warm water, and you unscrew it when you want to empty the bath. Then the water runs out into a bucket or something.'

'I know all that,' said Rosie. 'If you like you can fetch the water for the dolls' baths, and then empty it out of the tap when I've finished. You don't like playing with my dolls much, but you like doing things like that, don't you?'

'I don't mind,' said Sam, 'but I do think

you've got too many dolls, Rosie. Nobody has such a big family as you.'

'Yes, they really are a handful,' said Rosie proudly, looking round at all her dolls. 'I'm their mother, and you'd better be their father. Children like to have a mother *and* a father.'

'I'll be a father to the boy dolls,' said Sam. 'Not to the girl dolls. And I'll do any telling off when they're naughty. Fathers are useful for that.'

'You're not to tell off any of my children unless I say so,' said Rosie at once. 'They're very, very good children.'

'Only because they're not alive,' said Sam. 'They wouldn't always be good if they could really walk and talk and play.'

'Oh, I *wish* they could,' said Rosie. 'I'm always, always wishing that. Especially about Belinda.'

'Well, I'm always wishing my toy steam engine could *really* whistle and smoke, and that my toy cars could really be driven about,' said Sam. 'But it never happens!'

'Perhaps when there's magic about it will happen,' said Rosie. 'You never, never know!'

2

Mummy has some news

Sam and Rosie liked school, but they liked the holidays even better. Then they could go for long walks together – at least, Sam didn't walk, he rode on his bicycle. It was a lovely one, blue and silver.

Rosie walked because she always took her pram along with her, of course. She gave her dolls plenty of outings and they each had their turn in the big pram. 'I can take three or four of the smaller dolls,' she said, 'but when I take Big Belinda, there isn't room for anyone else. She's so very big.'

On rainy days they played down in their playroom. Rosie dressed and undressed the dolls, bathed them, pretended to feed them from a feeding bottle, and then tucked them up in cots. She had three cots: a tiny one, a bigger one that took four ordinary-sized dolls, and a very big one for Belinda.

Rosie was always busy on a rainy day. The children had a little sink in their playroom, and you should have seen the amount of washing that Rosie did there! She washed pyjamas, vests, dresses and socks, and even the cot blankets and sheets.

Mummy often smiled when she popped down to the playroom and saw Rosie busy washing at the little sink. There would be clothes hanging on a little line too, flapping in the wind. Sam had put up the line for Rosie at the bottom of the garden. He liked doing things like that.

'Mummy, I want to iron the things I've washed today,' said Rosie one day. 'They're so nice and clean and dry, but they look all wrinkled and crumpled because I haven't got an iron.'

'Well,' said Mummy, 'when Mrs Mills has had her cup of tea you can go into the kitchen and you can ask her to get the iron out. Then you can watch her while she does it for you.'

'Oh yes!' said Rosie.

'What about your toy iron and ironing board, Rosie?' said Sam. 'Why don't you get those out of the cupboard and do a bit of ironing yourself as well? Then you'll learn how to do it for when you're grown up.'

'Oh yes,' said Rosie, pleased.

Well, that meant that Rosie could watch Mrs Mills do all her ironing. Then she took it back to the playroom and ironed it all again by herself! For someone who was just seven years old, she really was a very good little mother.

Now one day Mummy called the children in. 'I've got to talk to you,' she said. 'I've something to tell you…'

They came over to her at once. 'Is Daddy coming home from his ship?' asked Sam, looking excited.

'No. Not for a long time, I'm afraid,' said Mummy, sadly. 'He's right on the other side of the world now. But he'll be home for Christmas. What I want to tell you is this. I'm going away for a few weeks, and Granny is coming to look after you, so…'

'Mummy, why are you going away?' cried Rosie in alarm. 'I don't like being without you. Don't go!'

'Listen, Rosie, I've got to have a rest, the doctor says,' said Mummy. 'But only for a few weeks. Then I'll be back again, as well as ever! And if you're good children and help dear Granny, I shall bring you back a most wonderful present.'

'What?' asked the children together. Mummy laughed.

'I shan't tell you yet. You wait and see,' she said. 'Now, will you help Granny all you can? She's a bit deaf now, so you'll have to speak nice and clearly. And she's got a bad foot, so she won't want to run up and down stairs too much.'

'We'll fetch everything for her,' said Rosie. 'We love Granny. She's kind and good fun. But you'll come back as soon as you can, won't you, Mummy? You do promise, don't you?'

'I promise faithfully,' said Mummy. 'Just as you promise faithfully to be good and helpful while I'm away. You will remember to do everything just as usual, won't you? Clean your teeth, wash your hands before meals, make your beds, say your prayers?'

'We won't forget *anything*,' said Sam, and Mummy knew they wouldn't. If Rosie forgot, Sam would remind her. He could always be trusted.

'I'll write to you and tell you my news and you can write and tell me yours,' said Mummy. 'So we'll know what everyone's doing. Now run away and play again.'

The children ran off to their playroom. Rosie looked rather solemn. 'I don't like Mummy going away,' she said. 'I don't like having Granny instead of Mummy.'

'Well, we can look forward to Mummy coming back,' said Sam, trying to think of something to cheer Rosie up. 'And Granny will make us some of that lovely nut toffee, and gingerbread men with little currant eyes and buttons down their coats. And she might even take us to the zoo.'

Rosie cheered up at once. 'Yes, I'd forgotten that lovely nut toffee. And anyway, Mummy hasn't gone yet.'

But, oh dear, Mummy went that very night,

11

while they were fast asleep in bed. In the morning when they went down for breakfast, there was Granny sitting at the table!

'What a surprise!' she said. 'I've come to stay with you!'

3

Granny comes to stay

The children missed Mummy very much. They missed hearing her quick footsteps tip-tapping here and there. They missed hearing her call out to them, 'Sam, Rosie, where are you? Come and taste my new buns!'

Granny didn't tip-tap about quickly. She had to walk slowly. She didn't call loudly to the children. Her voice was very quiet. She didn't like it when the next-door dog came bounding in to ask for a bone. She shooed him out at once.

But she was very, very kind. She had brought some big peppermints for them that lasted at least an hour each, if the children sucked them slowly. She had brought Rosie a lovely little brush and comb set for her dolls, and a new signal for Sam's railway.

After tea she read to them. They could both read well, but all the same they still liked being read to. Sometimes Granny told them things she had done long ago when she was as small as they were.

'Was there magic about when you were little, Granny?' asked Rosie. 'There doesn't seem to be any around now. Only in books.'

'Oh, there's magic if you look for it,' said Granny. 'How do you suppose a caterpillar goes to sleep and wakes up as a butterfly or moth? There's magic for you! And how does a great oak tree grow from a tiny little acorn? And what conjuror is clever enough to make a chicken grow inside an egg? There's magic everywhere.'

The children remembered what they'd promised Mummy. They ran up and down stairs for Granny, because she had a bad foot. They went down to the shops together whenever she asked them to. Sam found her knitting needle whenever she lost it; and she was always losing one of them!

Granny made them some nut toffee, of course, as the children had hoped she would.

There was a whole tin of it. 'There you are,' said Granny. 'That'll last us till Mummy comes back!'

Mrs Mills still came every day, but she went at tea time so the children always got the tea ready. Sam was allowed to switch the kettle on to boil, and Rosie spread the bread with some butter and set the little table just by Granny's chair.

'I must say, you're both very trustworthy children,' said Granny. 'I should get a shock if you were ever naughty.'

'Oh we are!' said Rosie. 'Mummy gets very cross sometimes. I bounced my ball in here last week and it knocked Mummy's little clock off the shelf and broke it. I nearly got sent to bed for that.'

'And I broke the cucumber frame by putting the watering can down on it when it was full of water,' said Sam. 'And I lost Daddy's best pen when he lent it to me. I simply couldn't tell you all the bad things we've done. But Mummy made us promise to be on our best behaviour with you, so I expect you think we're never naughty!'

15

'Well, if you can be good till tomorrow morning, I might make you some gingerbread men,' said Granny. 'I've found a packet of currants that'll do nicely for eyes and buttons. We'll have two gingerbread men each.'

So they did, though Rosie said it was a pity to eat such nice men. She fed two of her dolls with the crumbs. Granny always let her bring one or two of her 'children' to meals, so long as they behaved well. But when Sam made one doll kick a bun off the plate, that doll had to go and stand in the corner!

It was holiday time, so the children had plenty of time to play. One fine morning Rosie thought she would have a Grand Washing Day. Soon the sink in the playroom was full of hot soapy water, and the dolls' dirty clothes were being scrubbed and rinsed. Out they went on the little line, flapping in the wind. Mrs Mills saw them when she shook her duster out of the window, and she called to Granny, 'Just look at that, Mrs Barton! Isn't Rosie a proper little mother to her dolls? She'll be ironing those clothes this evening, you see if she won't!'

16

'Oh, she mustn't use the iron,' said Granny, quite shocked.

But Mrs Mills told her that the children's mother let Rosie watch the dolls' clothes being ironed. And then Rosie took them off to the playroom to be ironed all over again with the toy iron. So Granny watched when Rosie brought a basket of dolls' clothes down from the kitchen to be ironed in the playroom that evening. She watched Sam get the toy iron and ironing board ready for Rosie. She watched Rosie put the clothes one by one on the ironing board and iron them beautifully.

'Well, well!' said Granny. 'If you had a real live baby or two, you couldn't do better for them than you do for these dolls of yours. I never knew such a proper little mother as you!'

Rosie was pleased. 'I'm the mother and Sam's the father,' she said.

'Only the father of the boy dolls,' said Sam at once. 'The girl dolls have such silly faces.'

'They have *not*,' said Rosie, very cross. 'Anyway, what about the little man who drives your biggest toy car? He's got the silliest smile I've ever seen in all my life!'

'And you've got the crossest look *I've* ever seen,' said Granny, 'I hope you won't throw the iron at Sam. Now, what about a peppermint? It's about time we had one, I think. There's nothing like sucking a sweet when you want to say something cross!'

That made the children laugh. They took a peppermint each, and then Sam put the toy iron and ironing board away. 'Let's have a story, Granny,' he said, and they settled down for a good, long read.

4

Cuckoo Wood

Next day was very fine indeed. 'I think I'll take Big Belinda out for a walk,' said Rosie. 'Are you coming too, Sam?'

'Yes. I've cleaned my bicycle and it's longing for a trip,' said Sam. 'We'll go to Cuckoo Wood and look for some honeysuckle for Granny. It's the scent she likes best of all.'

Rosie and Sam went down to the playroom. The dolls sat around as usual, staring at the children as they came in. Rosie went to where her biggest doll was sitting up in her cot.

'You're going for a walk,' she said. 'I'll just sponge your face and hands, and brush your hair with the brush Granny gave me. Then I'll put on your new bonnet, and tuck you up in the pram!'

She sponged Big Belinda's face and hands. Belinda sat and smiled. She always smiled, even when she lay down and shut her eyes. Rosie hugged her.

'You're lovely and big and quite soft, but you don't feel *warm* like all real babies do,' she said. 'If only you'd come alive, just for once. Still, you really are a lovely baby doll. Now, let me brush your hair.'

Belinda had hair like a real baby's. It was short and soft and curly. Rosie brushed it till it shone. Then she tied Belinda's little white bonnet under her chin.

'Now you're ready for your pram,' she said. She went to where she kept the pram, over in the corner, and turned back the covers. They were all clean and tidy. Rosie shook up the little white pillow and then laid Belinda down in the pram.

'Now I'll cover you up,' she said. 'I think you ought to go to sleep, because you've been sitting up for a long time. That's right. Shut your eyes and you'll soon be asleep.'

Sam rang his bicycle bell impatiently outside the playroom door. 'Rosie! Aren't you coming yet? I've been waiting for ages!'

'Don't keep ringing your bell. You'll wake up Belinda,' said Rosie. 'I'm only just ready. Wow! Doesn't your bicycle look bright and shiny! You *have* cleaned it well.'

'Yes, haven't I?' said Sam, pleased, and he rode off down the path that led to the gate in the nearby wall. He opened it and let Rosie go through with her big doll's pram. Then he followed on his shining bicycle.

They went down the road, through a field gate and across a meadow to the other side. Up a hill they walked, and down a lane, and then they came to Cuckoo Wood.

'We'll take this path,' said Rosie. 'Then Belinda can sleep properly. You go on ahead, Sam, and I'll follow.'

They went a little way into the wood. Mummy always said that they must still be able to see the swings whenever they went to Cuckoo Wood by themselves. 'Never go on your own,' said Mummy. 'Always go together.' They knew the wood well because they went so often. They knew where the biggest black-berries grew in September, and where the hazelnuts ripened in October. They knew

21

where the first primroses peeped up by the hazel trees, and where the bluebells shone like blue pools in May. It really was a lovely wood.

'Now let's go and look for honeysuckle,' said Rosie. She put her pram beside a wooden seat near an oak tree and slipped on the brake so that it couldn't run away. She was always very careful with her dolls.

Sam put his bicycle behind a bush. The children were going to scramble through the bushes to find the honeysuckle, and the bicycle wouldn't be of any use for that.

Off they went. 'I'm sure I remember where we found the honeysuckle last year,' said Sam. 'Down here. Look! And then round by that beech, and over a little stream, and look! There's the honeysuckle!'

They jumped the stream and ran to where the honeysuckle twined itself over a big bush. It smelt very sweet as Rosie sniffed all the tiny yellow trumpets.

'Lovely!' she said. 'Let's hunt round for some more.'

They had a fine time in the woods. Every now and again Rosie turned round and checked. Yes! She could still see the swings. They saw two grey squirrels and crouched down behind a bush to watch them. They saw a baby rabbit scurrying about like a little mad thing. They found some lizards on a bank and sat down quietly to watch them play.

'Hey, do you think it's getting late?' said Sam suddenly. 'I feel so hungry.'

'So do I,' said Rosie. 'Yes, I think it must be late. We'd better be going home. Come on, let's go back and fetch the pram and your bicycle.'

Back they went, over the stream, round by the big beech tree and through the bushes. And there, near the wooden seat where it had been left, was Rosie's pram. Behind the bush was the bicycle.

'Come on,' said Rosie, pushing the pram. 'I won't wait to sit Belinda up. I expect she's still asleep. Let's go quickly.'

They went down the path, with Sam in front on his bicycle. Rosie panted as she pushed her pram.

'Sam,' she called. 'I can't go as fast as you. Wait for me!' She bumped over a hole in the path and the pram jerked and jolted.

Rosie stopped. 'I'll have to have a little rest,' she said. 'Please wait for me, Sam.'

So Sam got off his bike and leaned it against a tree.

'Listen!' he said suddenly. 'Did you hear that?'

Rosie listened. 'No,' she said. Then, after a moment, she heard it too. 'Yes, I can now,' she said.

It was a strange, crying sort of noise. And it seemed to be coming from behind the bushes. Whatever could it be?

5

A very strange thing

'Come on,' said Sam, 'let's go and have a look.'

But Rosie hung back. 'You go,' she said, holding onto the pram tightly. Then she heard it again – a sad, weak little whining noise. Sam dived round the side of the tree and burrowed into some bushes beyond it. 'It must be an animal in pain,' he called, his voice muffled.

Rosie waited. 'Hurry up, Sam!' she said at last. 'Do be careful. The poor creature might bite you if it's hurt.'

'Rosie!' shouted Sam at last. 'Rosie, you'll never guess! Come here at once!'

Rosie took a look round and made sure she could still see the swings. She checked the brake on her pram. And then, a little bit scared, she began to walk round the tree.

Suddenly Sam crawled out of the under-growth. He was carrying something in his arms very carefully. He scrambled to his feet. Rosie ran forward to have a look. 'Sam,' she said, 'what on earth have you got? Is it a…?'

Sam cradled the creature gently in his arms. 'Yes,' he whispered. 'It's a puppy. A dear, dear little puppy. And I think he's lost and fright-ened and very tired.'

The two children gazed at the puppy with-out speaking. His little black nose was resting on Sam's arm and his eyes were tight shut. He breathed in deeply and gave a little snore, and then he settled down again. 'He's fast asleep,' said Rosie.

'Yes,' said Sam. 'Now that I've rescued him he must feel safe and so he's having a snooze!' Sam stared at the puppy. 'He's a bit dirty,' he said. 'And his coat is all muddy and matted. This is really strange, Rosie. I can't think what has happened.'

'He's somehow got lost,' said Rosie. 'He must have got separated from his mother and wandered off. Perhaps he tried to find her.'

'Yes,' said Sam, 'and he ended up in the

undergrowth, quite lost. And honestly, Rosie, he's rather heavy. My arms are aching.'

Rosie stroked his head gently. 'What a lovely black and white coat,' she said. 'Or it would be if I could only wash and brush him.' Then she said excitedly, 'Sam, it's just as if my wishes have come true! I know I wished I could have a live doll. Belinda's still ... well, Belinda, my big Baby doll. But look! We've got a real live puppy to look after instead! My wish has come true in a strange way, hasn't it? It's fantastic!'

'But Rosie, what are we going to do with this, this little puppy?' asked Sam, frowning. 'We really can't keep a puppy at home. That would be impossible.'

'Why not?' asked Rosie, patting the puppy. 'He's ours. I can wash him and put him into Belinda's cot, and we can take him for walks.'

'What about feeding him?' asked Sam. 'And how will you know what to feed him on?'

'I shall feed him just like Mr Williams fed those puppies we saw last week,' said Rosie, remembering their visit to the vet and his nurse, Miss Morgan. 'Our puppy's just the same size as those puppies we saw. So he can

27

have cereal and milk and some tins of puppy food. Miss Morgan told me all about it.'

'You can't, Rosie,' said Sam. 'Anyway, whatever will Granny say? She wouldn't let you keep him.'

Rosie looked quite determined. 'I shan't say anything to Granny about it, or to *anyone*,' she said. 'This puppy is my wish come true. He's ours. If we tell Granny, she won't understand how I feel. Grown-ups often don't. Oh, Sam, don't tell her, will you? I couldn't bear him to be taken away from us.'

'Don't cry,' said Sam, seeing tears suddenly come into Rosie's eyes. 'I won't tell. I promise. But HOW are we going to keep this puppy to ourselves? We can't take him into the house.'

'I'm not going to,' said Rosie, smiling at him. 'He's going to live where Belinda lives, down in the playroom.'

'I see,' said Sam, beginning to feel excited. 'Rosie, what a *wonderful* secret we've got!'

'I shall look after him, and feed him, and bath him, and put him to sleep,' said Rosie, happily. 'It's what I've always wanted, a real living thing to look after. And now my wish has come true, and we're going to keep him for our very own.'

'Well, we'd better get back home,' said Sam. 'Or Granny'll be looking out for us, and if the puppy's whining she'll find out about it at once!' Then he looked round. 'My arms are aching,' he said.

'I know,' said Rosie, 'look.'

She put the puppy into her doll's pram. He was bigger and heavier than Belinda, but he fitted in quite nicely. She tucked him in carefully. He was still fast asleep.

'Have a lovely sleep,' said Rosie softly, and patted him. 'You're quite safe. You've come to your new "Mummy" now and she'll look after you. You belong to us.'

So they set off. Sam rode in front on his bicycle. Rosie pushed the pram behind. At last they came to their garden gate. Rosie pushed the pram quietly up the little path to the playroom. Sam opened the door and Rosie went inside with the pram. Almost at once he heard the voice of Mrs Mills. 'Is that you children back again? You're late. Your Granny says come along in to dinner at once.'

They rushed up to the house with the honeysuckle they'd picked for Granny. Just in time! And, oh, what a secret they had! What a strange and wonderful secret!

6

Down in the playroom

Granny couldn't think why the children were so red in the face and had such shining eyes at dinner time. 'You look as if you've been up to mischief!' she said, laughing. 'What have you been doing?'

'We've been for a walk in the woods,' said Sam. 'At least, Rosie walked and I went on my bicycle. We had a lovely time. I'm sorry we were late. It was all, well, very exciting.'

'Would you like to go out to tea with Emma this afternoon?' asked Granny. 'I met her mother this morning and she said you could go to tea if you liked.'

The children looked at each other in alarm. How could they possibly go out to tea and leave the puppy alone in the playroom?

'I don't think we'll go out to tea today,' said Rosie. 'I don't feel like it, Granny.'

Granny was surprised, but she didn't ask any questions. She just thought that the children had some plans of their own. And that was quite true, of course!

'Very well,' she said. 'I'll telephone Emma's mother and say you can't go. Will you be down in the playroom all afternoon? If so, I think I'll lie down and have a rest in a few minutes. I went for a rather long walk this morning.'

'Yes. We'll be down there,' said Rosie. 'Do you think we could have our tea down there today, Granny? Mrs Mills said she was going to be here till after tea, so she could get yours, couldn't she? We could take some milk and biscuits and a piece of cake down with us.'

'Yes, do that,' said Granny. 'I might pop along to Emma's mother later and have tea with her. She asked me as well as you. You sound as if you're going to be very busy, my dears.'

'Oh yes we are!' said Rosie. 'We're going to have a lovely time.'

The children ran down to the playroom as soon as they could. There wasn't a sound to be heard as they opened the door. Rosie looked at Sam.

'Sam, I do hope the puppy's all right. He might be feeling lost and missing his mother.'

'Yes,' said Sam, who was still feeling very puzzled. How could anyone lose a puppy? But then perhaps everyone felt puzzled and bewildered when amazing things really happened.

They went in and shut the door. Rosie tiptoed over to the cot and bent down. Then she looked round at Sam in delight, her eyes shining.

'The puppy's still here. Look, he's asleep. He's breathing – you can see the blanket moving up and down. Look at his tiny paw with its little claws. Isn't he sweet?'

'He's still rather dirty,' said Sam. 'When are you going to wash him?'

'I think we'd better get a bowl of water ready first, because he'll be thirsty when he wakes up,' said Rosie.

Sam looked around for a bowl. 'Can we use the sugar bowl from your dolls' tea set?' he asked.

'Well, it's a bit small, but I expect it'll do for now,' said Rosie.

'I'd better wash it out and put in some water,' said Sam. 'And we'll get the same puppy food that Miss Morgan uses. The puppies she was looking after were so plump and jolly that I'm sure it must be good food.'

'Will you go and buy a tin for me please, Sam? Then I'll get a meal ready and feed the puppy.'

'But don't puppies eat special biscuits as well, mixed in with their meat?' asked Sam, looking worried. 'And what about the money? Will it cost a lot?'

'I don't know. We'll have to see how much we've got in our money boxes,' said Rosie. 'We've got quite a lot, I know that. Can you go and get them, Sam, please?'

Sam fetched the money boxes and emptied the money onto the table. Out came some pennies, some ten and twenty pence pieces, five fifty pence pieces and four pound coins.

'You must put some in your pocket,' said Rosie. 'And you'd better buy some milk as well. Can you go to the pet shop at the end of the village street, in case the one nearby starts asking you awkward questions?'

'Good idea, Rosie,' said Sam. 'You think of everything! All right, I'll go now. Look, the puppy's waking up.'

So he was. He opened his eyes. He yawned very widely indeed and rubbed his nose with his paw. Rosie slipped her finger under his tummy and the puppy snuggled up to her. It was a lovely feeling. Rosie lifted up the puppy. 'You do want a bath,' she said. 'And as soon as Sam gets back we'll give you one, even though I don't know how often puppies are supposed to have baths! Now you lie quietly in my arms until Sam comes back.'

But the puppy didn't. He was hungry and he began to whimper and whine and struggle. He sounded so miserable that Rosie was quite upset. She rocked him and patted him, hoping that Sam wouldn't be too long. His hair was very black, with some white patches, and in fact he had a white patch between his eyes. 'Just like a star,' thought Rosie. Then she thought, excited, 'That would be a good name for him! Let's call him Star!'

Sam came back at last with two tins of puppy meat, a new bowl, a bag of puppy biscuits and a bottle of milk. 'The man in the pet shop said we ought to put plenty of newspapers down,' he said. 'He told me that puppies can take a few weeks to train properly.'

'That's a good idea,' said Rosie. 'Would you like to hold the puppy? I'll go and look in the kitchen cupboard. Mummy keeps a pile of old newspapers there.'

But, oh dear! The children began to feel a bit worried. Suppose they didn't look after the puppy properly?

7

Looking after the puppy

It took quite a long time to read all the directions on the tin of puppy meat, to mix it with the biscuits and then add a drop of warm water. The puppy got hungrier than ever and began to wriggle, sniffing hard. But as soon as Rosie put the bowl of food near his mouth, he stopped wriggling and began to lick at the food.

'Look, he's beginning to eat his food already,' said Rosie, delighted. 'Oh, Sam, I've often pretended I was feeding Belinda out of her little feeding bottle, but this is much more exciting! Look, he's finished it all now. Do you want to hold him for a minute?'

'No thanks!' said Sam. 'I'll just watch. When are you going to wash him, Rosie?'

'Well, I thought I'd get on with it now he's finished his dinner.'

But when the puppy had licked round his bowl all over again and lapped up some water from the dolls' sugar bowl, he began to walk round the playroom, sniffing rather determinedly.

'I think he needs to go out,' said Sam suddenly. 'Quick, Rosie, open the door.'

Rosie flew to the door and opened it just in time.

'Suppose Granny or Mrs Mills see him on the grass?' said Sam, anxiously. But soon the puppy had finished and began to wag his tail.

'Come here!' cried Rosie. The puppy didn't seem to know what 'Come here!' meant, though, and he trotted off across the lawn in the direction of the flower beds. Sam ran and caught him quickly and brought him back into the playroom.

'I think I'd better wash the pram sheets and blankets,' said Rosie, 'and hang them out in the sunshine. Then you can make him a bed and I'll give him a bath.'

No sooner had Sam put the cot mattress under the window than the puppy ran up to

him on his stumpy little legs, gave him a lick
and then lay down on the mattress in the sun.
He was soon fast asleep. Rosie covered him up
and he grunted a little.

'He sounded just like a little pig then,' said
Sam anxiously. 'You don't think he'll change
into a piglet, do you Rosie?'

'No I don't!' said Rosie. 'Don't be silly, Sam.
Do you think you could go and buy him a
lead? We can take him out for walks then.'

'*You* go and buy it,' said Sam. 'Let me stay
with the puppy this time. I'm tired of walking
up and down the hill to the pet shop.'

'Well, you're not much good as a father!'
said Rosie. 'Real fathers don't mind things like
that. Anyway, I'll go. I might think of something else.'

So Rosie went off to the shops and Sam was
left with the puppy. He sat and stared at him.
It was all very, very extraordinary; rather like
a dream. Perhaps it *was* a dream. But it could-
n't be, because Rosie was having the same
dream, so it must be real.

'Pity I haven't been wishing that my engine
could really whistle and smoke,' thought Sam.

'If Rosie's wish could come true, there's no reason why mine shouldn't too.'

Then the puppy woke up. He opened his eyes and, to Sam's horror, he began to howl very loudly. 'Sh!' said Sam, patting him. 'Sh! What's the matter? Sh! You'll have Mrs Mills here in a minute!'

To his horror he saw Mrs Mills in the distance, hanging out some tea towels on the line near the kitchen door.

'Yow … yow … yow!' howled the puppy. Mrs Mills turned her head and in despair, Sam picked the puppy up from the mattress and held him in his arms. The puppy stopped howling at once and began to wriggle. Mrs Mills went back indoors.

'Honestly! You nearly gave our secret away!' said Sam to the puppy. 'And you do feel rather nice! You feel more like a warm teddy bear than a live puppy, all soft and cuddly. I rather like you!'

'Wuff!' said the puppy suddenly, in a tiny, high-pitched bark. He looked as if he was smiling at Sam. Sam gave him a hug that made him gasp.

'Sorry,' said Sam. 'But you really are rather nice! Look! Stop licking my face! Help! There's someone coming.'

Before Sam could put the puppy back onto the mattress, the playroom door opened. But it was only Rosie – and wasn't she surprised to see Sam cuddling the puppy!

'I thought you didn't want to hold him,' she said. 'He does feel nice, doesn't he? Look, I've got a lead. Let's have our tea and then bath the puppy. I'm simply longing to do that!'

'He's been howling,' said Sam. 'I don't know why.'

'Well,' said Rosie, 'I saw a programme on television about dogs. And they do howl sometimes, if they're calling for their parents or brothers and sisters.'

'Poor little thing,' said Sam. 'He must be feeling lonely.'

But the puppy didn't look lonely at all. He sat up in Sam's arms, gave him a lick, struggled to get free and then ran round and round the playroom, wagging his tail!

8

What a lovely secret!

It was fun to have a real live puppy to bath. Even Sam thought it was exciting. Rosie gave him quite a lot of jobs to do.

'Can you put the plastic bath on its stand?' she said. 'Over there, away from the draught. And put some cold water in the bath and then add some hot water. You *always* have to pour the cold water in first, so the puppy won't get scalded.'

Sam put the bath on its stand. He filled it with lukewarm water, a mixture of cold and hot. He went indoors to get some soap from Rosie's bedroom. He found a towel in the airing cupboard too, a smooth, soft one.

Nobody saw him. Mrs Mills had gone and Granny was out. He went back to Rosie, who had now picked up the puppy. He whined a little, and the children laughed.

'He's happy,' said Rosie, pleased. 'Look, Puppy! See your nice bath? In you go!'

Into the bath went the puppy. He gasped when he felt the water, but he didn't make a fuss. He kicked a little and splashed Rosie. She knew exactly how to hold him, with one hand firmly under his fat little tummy. She bathed him well while Sam watched.

'He's a lot cleaner now,' he said. 'Shall I do his feet?'

'All right,' said Rosie. She really wanted to do each tiny claw herself, but she thought Sam ought to have a turn. So he washed the puppy's feet, and the little thing whined again and wriggled.

'Now I'll lift him out and dry him,' said Rosie. 'Aren't we getting on well! Can you empty the bath water and clean the bath and put it away, Sam?'

He nodded and set to work. Rosie dried the little black and white creature and then spent a happy minute cuddling him in the towel. Sam watched her. He had turned on the tap under the bath to let the water run out, and he was waiting for the bath to empty. Rosie looked up and gave a squeal.

'Oh Sam! Look what you've done! You've turned the tap on and let the water out, but you haven't put a bucket underneath to catch the water! It's running all over the floor!'

So it was. What a mess! Poor Sam spent the next twenty minutes mopping up the floor. By that time Rosie had dried the puppy all over. She brushed and combed his straight soft hair with an old doll's hair brush and comb, and then she cuddled him and sang him a little song.

'Sam,' she said at last. 'I just don't understand why my wishes suddenly came true. But they have, haven't they? This isn't a dream, is it? I do feel so happy.'

'I wouldn't mop up water in a dream,' said Sam, who was feeling rather cross and wet. 'Are you going to give the puppy a drink of milk? Let me hold him while you get the bowl ready.'

He held him on his knee. The puppy felt warm and comfortable. He licked Sam, and Sam tickled him.

'I like this puppy,' he said to Rosie. 'He isn't dirty any more and he smells nice now. But don't you think we ought to tell someone, Rosie? How long do you think we'll be able to keep him?'

'Oh no, don't let's tell anyone just yet!' said Rosie, who was busy getting the bowl of milk. 'I love my doll Belinda, but a real *puppy* is so much nicer. We can easily keep him down here. We could ask Mrs Mills to let us know when she wants to clean our playroom, and we could go off for the day with the puppy in the pram. Then no one will guess.'

'Yes, we could do that,' said Sam. 'But what will Mummy say when she comes back? We should give him back really, shouldn't we? Suppose he belongs to another family who are missing him?'

'I haven't thought as far as that,' said Rosie. 'But let's just look after him for a bit longer, Sam.'

She put the bowl of milk on the playroom floor and the puppy came and lapped up a little. He couldn't finish it all this time, but Rosie didn't think that would matter. She laid him down gently on the mattress under the window. He really did fit on it very well and he was such a good little thing. He yawned widely and then shut his eyes.

'He's off to sleep already,' said Sam. 'Rosie, what's going to happen if he wakes up and barks in the night?'

'I'd thought of that,' said Rosie. 'I'm going to sleep down here with him. I can curl up on that old sofa over there. No one will know. Granny doesn't come up to our rooms to kiss us goodnight because her bad foot doesn't like the stairs. So she won't know I'm down here.'

'I'll come too,' said Sam. 'I'd like to. I could bring in the cushions from the swing-seat in the garden. They'd make a great bed.'

'All right,' said Rosie. 'You do that. It'll be fun. But now I'm going to start on the washing. Everything got damp in the pram and Belinda's clothes have got a bit dirty too.'

She started straightaway. All the sheets, blankets and doll's clothes went into the hot soapy water in the little sink. How Rosie scrubbed and rubbed and rinsed. Then out on the line they went.

The puppy slept peacefully. Sam and Rosie tidied up the room and then took out books to read. They hoped that Granny wouldn't come to look for them!

'I'll just see if the washing is dry enough to iron,' said Rosie at last. Out she went and then popped her head back in through the door.

'It's just right. I'll go and ask Mrs Mills, like Mummy said I could. She'll think I've been washing Belinda's clothes again!'

'All right,' said Sam. 'I'll get out your toy iron and ironing board and put them up in the corner of the playroom for you.'

Soon Rosie was busy with Mrs Mills and the ironing. How happy she was. What a secret she had! She could hardly believe it was true. And although she knew they would have to give the puppy back one day, she squashed that thought right to the back of her mind.

9

At night

Granny found Rosie watching Mrs Mills ironing away in the kitchen. Granny laughed. 'Well,
well! Have you had another washing day for
your dolls? What a good little mother you are!'

'I like it,' said Rosie. 'Granny, did you have
a nice time at Emma's? Can I do anything for
you? We've hardly seen you all day.'

'You can just see if you can find one of my
knitting needles for me,' said Granny. 'I've lost
it again!'

Rosie soon found it. She looked at Granny's
knitting. 'Are you knitting a baby's blanket?'
she said. 'I think *I* ought to learn how to knit
too. Who's the blanket for, Granny?'

'For a little creature I haven't seen yet,' said
Granny, and smiled.

Rosie stared at her. Did Granny know about the baby puppy in the playroom, then? Whatever did she mean? The blanket looked just the right size for him, but if Granny had never seen the puppy she wouldn't know how big he was, would she?

'Maybe I'll teach you how to knit,' said Granny. 'It's so easy, and very useful when there's a baby about.'

Rosie was sure that Granny had guessed about the puppy. What on earth was going to happen? Would Granny begin to ask awkward questions? Rosie decided to go out of the room before that happened.

She ran down to the playroom. 'I think Granny knows something about the puppy,' she said. 'I hope she doesn't come and look.'

'He's fast asleep,' said Sam. 'Don't you think we'd better go to bed now, in case Granny makes up her mind to come and fetch us? We can easily slip back down here again when we hear her put the television on at half past eight.'

The children went up to the house, leaving the puppy sleeping peacefully. They had their supper, which Mrs Mills had left ready for them: milk, stewed plums and biscuits. Then they kissed Granny goodnight and went upstairs to get undressed.

When they heard the television go on at half past eight, down the stairs they crept again, dressed in their night things, taking their clothes with them for the morning. Granny didn't hear a thing!

The puppy still slept soundly. 'Will he want a drink at ten o'clock?' whispered Sam. 'And one early in the morning? Most *human* babies do.'

'I'll leave everything ready, in case,' said Rosie. 'I hope those garden cushions won't be too uncomfortable, Sam.'

They soon fell asleep. The puppy slept all through the night until nearly six o'clock. Then he woke up and howled dismally. Rosie leaped up at once.

'Oh no! How loud he sounds! He must be calling for his mother! Sam, pick him up while I get his milk and puppy biscuits ready.'

'This must be what Mummy and Daddy had to do for us when we were tiny,' said Sam, rocking the puppy up and down. 'Honestly, it's quite good fun. Sh! Star! You'll wake everyone up!' Then the puppy wriggled to be let down. He ran to the corner and made a puddle.

'Why didn't you put him outside?' asked Rosie, crossly.

'I was scared he'd make a noise,' said Sam, putting him back on his mattress.

It didn't seem worthwhile to try to go back to sleep again after all that, so the children got dressed and then wiped up the puddle. Sam decided to stay with the puppy while Rosie went back to the house to brush her hair and see if Granny was awake. She often woke very early and made herself a cup of tea. Today Rosie decided to do it for her.

'Oh! You are an early bird this morning!' said Granny when she heard a knock at her door at quarter past seven, and Rosie came in carrying a plate of biscuits and a mug of tea on a tray. 'Stay and have a biscuit with me,' said Granny.

Granny wondered where the children disappeared to so quickly after breakfast. They were off and away at once, because Rosie thought she heard the puppy whining.

'He's longing for his bath,' she said to Sam. Sam didn't think so. He didn't think the puppy looked used to having baths at all. Still, Rosie badly wanted to bath him again, so they made a start.

'I don't really think we ought to give him so many baths,' said Sam. 'I don't think puppies have lots of baths.'

'Oh, just this once,' said Rosie and so Sam agreed.

After the bath the puppy wanted to play. He raced round and round the playroom like a mad thing. He found an old ball of Sam's and pushed it along with his nose, yelping and barking in excitement.

'Sh! Sh!' cried Rosie, but it was no good. The more they tried to kick the ball away the more the puppy raced and yelped. At last, however, he flopped down, panting. Sam decided to clear up the bath water. This time Sam remembered to put a bucket under the bath when he turned on the tap to empty out the water.

'Rosie! Granny's coming down the path! Look!' said Sam suddenly. 'Put the puppy in the pram, quick!'

Much to his surprise, the puppy was put into the doll's pram in a great hurry, and was tucked in so well that only the top of his head showed. Rosie didn't dare let his little black and white face show!

Granny opened the door and looked round. 'So here you are!' she said. 'What are you two doing down here all the time? It must be something very interesting to make you spend so much time on it.'

'Well ... we've got all our toys down here, Granny,' said Sam.

The puppy clearly felt too tightly wrapped up and gave a whine. Granny looked startled. 'What was that?' she said, looking round.

Sam picked up a teddy bear and Rosie snatched up a toy cat that mewed when you pulled a string. The bear growled as Sam pressed his middle and the cat mewed. Granny laughed.

'Oh, it's your toy animals, I suppose. Just for a moment I thought it sounded like a puppy whining. But there! My ears aren't as good as they used to be. Would you like to show me all your dolls?'

'Oh no!' thought Rosie. 'This is awful!'

Then she heard Mrs Mills calling Granny. 'Are you there, Mrs Barton? There's someone on the phone.' And away went Granny up the path. Their secret was safe. What a narrow escape!

10

Big worries – and a shock

For the next few days the children had a very exciting time. They looked after the puppy well, fed him, played with him on the grass and in the playroom, and gave him drinks of water. In fact they did everything they should.

They took him out in the pram each day, well covered up. They went down quiet lanes and into the corner of a field, afraid that perhaps the puppy might wake up and bark. Then someone would hear him and be quite amazed. They tried to teach him how to go for a walk on a lead, but the puppy didn't like that and tried to chew the lead instead.

'The puppy has got used to us now, hasn't he?' said Sam. 'I didn't think real live puppies could be such fun. I think he's grown already, don't you?'

'Oh, don't say that!' said Rosie, in alarm. 'If he grows much more we won't be able to fit him into the pram or the cot!'

'What's going to happen when he grows?' said Sam. 'I mean, he's going to start being a grown-up dog one day, isn't he?'

'I suppose so,' said Rosie, looking worried. 'Don't let's talk about that now, Sam. I want things to stay as they are. This is our secret. He belongs to us and I don't want anyone else to see him or share him. It's a wish come true!'

'But Rosie…' said Sam.

Rosie just put her hands over her ears.

Then there was another worry for Sam and Rosie. Sam was going to go shopping for some more tins of puppy food and some more bis-cuits. He came to Rosie.

'Rosie! We've got hardly any money left in our money boxes. What on earth are we going to do?'

'But we had loads,' said Rosie, in dismay.

'I know, but we've *spent* loads as well,' said

Sam. 'I don't think we've got enough to buy the tins of puppy food.'

'Go and look in my top drawer in the bedroom,' said Rosie. 'I might have a few coins there.'

Sam went to look, but there was no money there at all. He felt very gloomy. Could he do some work and get paid for it? That's what real fathers did to buy food for their children.

As he went downstairs Granny called him. 'Is that you, Sam? Will you go and fetch me some more wool from the wool shop? And ask for my paper at the newsagent's?'

'Yes, of course,' said Sam, and he went into the lounge where Granny was sitting knitting. She fumbled for her purse.

'There's the money for the wool, and the paper. And this two pound coin is for you and Rosie. You can buy ice-creams or sweets with it if you'd like.'

'Oh, thank you, Granny,' said Sam in delight. Fantastic! Now they had enough money to buy whatever Rosie wanted for the puppy. What a brilliant piece of luck!

Soon they'd had the puppy for over a week.

They slept in the playroom at night and nobody knew. They looked after the puppy well and he loved them. He was a hungry little creature and ate up his breakfast and his dinner, and drank his milk to the last drop.

'A puppy isn't a bit of trouble, really,' said Rosie. 'If only we had more money, Sam! Do you think we'll have to tell Granny the next time we want to buy something else for him and haven't any money?'

'She won't be very pleased to think we've kept it all such a secret,' said Sam. 'Perhaps it wasn't such a very good idea to keep it all to ourselves.'

'It was, it was!' said Rosie. 'It's been the loveliest secret in the world! Oh, Sam, suppose they took the puppy away and we didn't have him to love any more? I would miss him dreadfully.'

Later that morning their cousins, John and Sarah, came round and knocked on the playroom door.

'Hello you two!' said Sam, 'It's lovely to see you, now you've come back from your holidays.'

'We've got a secret,' said Rosie. 'The best secret in the world!'

'Whatever do you mean?' asked Sarah.

'Well,' said Sam, 'we were in Cuckoo Wood one day and were coming back along the path, and we heard something whining…'

Just at that moment the puppy sat up on his mattress, shook himself, whined, and then ran as fast as he could and leaped onto Sam, licking his face and nearly knocking him over!

'What on earth is that?' cried John.

'It's our puppy,' said Rosie proudly. 'We thought we'd call him Star.'

Soon all the children were rolling round the playroom floor, while the puppy threw himself in among them, barking delightedly and licking them all in turn.

'Wow!' said John. 'He's fantastic, isn't he?'

'He's lovely,' said Sarah. 'When did your Mummy get him for you?'

Sam looked at Rosie, and Rosie looked at Sam.

'Er … she didn't exactly *get* him for us,' said Sam.

'But we found him!' said Rosie proudly. 'And now we're looking after him.'

'Do you mean until the owners come for him?' asked Sarah. 'And what does your Mummy say?'

'Well, nothing really,' said Sam, in a small, worried voice.

'Mummy's not here,' said Rosie. 'Granny's looking after us.'

Sarah said slowly, 'Aunty Sue doesn't know, does she? You haven't told your Mummy *or* your Granny!'

At that moment the puppy sniffed at the ball and began to push it round the playroom floor with his little damp, black nose. The more he pushed, the more he whined and barked in excitement, and the more he wagged his tail.

'Oh, look at him, the darling,' said Rosie. 'He's playing football!'

'Sh! Sh! Sh!' said Sam. 'Granny'll hear him.'

John picked up the puppy and cuddled him. The puppy planted a big wet lick on his cheek. 'He's lovely,' said John. 'And he's the most fantastic secret, Rosie, he really is. I don't blame

you for wanting to keep him, but you see...'
He gave Sarah a worried look.

'Before we came here we went down to the
village for some sweets at the newsagent's,'
said Sarah. 'In fact we got you two some as
well.' She gave Sam and Rosie a packet each.
'On the way back we walked past the post
office and we noticed a sign in the window.
There was a photo of a little black and white
puppy, just like Star.'

'And underneath,' said John, 'it said,
"Beautiful collie puppy lost. Please contact Mr
and Mrs Smith and Paul and Jane if you find
him. We miss him dreadfully."'

Sam and Rosie stared in horror at their
cousins. 'Lost?' said Sam. 'A black and white
puppy?'

'Yes,' said John. 'We've written down the
phone number.'

Rosie began to cry. 'I can't give him back,'
she sobbed. 'I love him.'

'But the other boy and girl must love him too,'
said Sam. 'We'll have to give him back, Rosie.'

Rosie hung her head. 'I don't think I can eat
these sweets now,' she said.

63

The four cousins looked at one another. Whatever were they going to do?

'I know,' said Rosie. 'If we give him back tomorrow, will that be all right? Then I can keep him just one more night!'

John and Sarah nodded. 'Yes. But you must take him to the vet's first thing tomorrow morning, Rosie. Then he can telephone Mr and Mrs Smith and tell them their puppy's been found.'

Rosie and Sam nodded. 'Yes. We'll do that,' said Sam.

'We'd better get back now,' said John, looking at his watch. 'Mummy'll be wondering where we've got to.'

So the two cousins went back home and left Sam and Rosie in the playroom.

'Come on,' said Sam. 'Cheer up, Rosie, and don't worry now. It's a lovely day, so why don't we take him for a walk? At least we can enjoy that one more time.'

'Oh yes!' said Rosie. 'I'll get ready straightaway.'

'Come along,' she said, pushing the pram down the path. 'Today we'll take you back to where we found you. It's nice and quiet there. We'll have a lovely time near the swings and Cuckoo Wood.'

But they didn't. Something awful happened. Just as they went down the path to the corner of the wood, two tall, dark-haired children stood in their way. They looked worried and sad, and as they were passing the puppy suddenly barked quite loudly.

'Let me look in your pram,' said the girl suddenly, and she tore off the covers roughly. The puppy stared up in surprise.

'Yes!' said the girl and the boy. 'You've got our puppy! We've been looking for him every day for a week. You give him back to us at once! How dare you take our puppy away?'

What a terrible shock for Sam and Rosie! Were these the puppy's real owners? Whatever did they mean?

11

Everything goes wrong

Sam and Rosie stared at the two older children in great alarm. Rosie tried to cover up the puppy again. He was struggling and whining.

'We're going to have our puppy back,' said the girl, and she threw back the covers once more and picked up the puppy. She nursed him against her and he stopped whimpering and began to wag his tail.

'See? He knows me,' said the girl. 'You really are naughty children to take him away!'

'But ... but ... we didn't know he belonged to anyone,' said Rosie, beginning to cry. 'We came here to the corner of this wood with Big Belinda, my doll, in the pram and we left her in the pram while we went to get some honeysuckle.'

'And when we got back and decided to go home, we heard a whining in the woods,' said Sam. 'I went into the bushes and found the puppy. He was tired and frightened and went to sleep in my arms.'

'Well,' said the big boy, 'we'd been to the swings on our way to going out for a picnic. The puppy came with us and he kept racing round and round and barking. All of a sudden Mummy and Daddy came past in the car. They stopped and called to us to hurry up. So I snatched up one bag of sandwiches and Jane, my sister, picked up the other.

'I thought Paul had the puppy,' said Jane, 'and he thought I'd got him. As soon as we realized he was missing we rushed back to find him.'

'We'd only been gone about five minutes,' said Paul. 'But although we searched and searched, and called and called, we never found him. Mummy and Daddy were very cross with us.'

'And we weren't allowed to go on the picnic either,' said Jane. 'We've been hunting for him all week. It's been awful. Nobody could tell us where he was!' Her eyes filled with tears.

'Oh dear!' said Rosie, still crying herself. 'I'm so sorry. You must have missed that darling puppy so much. I thought it was my wish come true, and that I'd been given a real live creature to look after, as well as Belinda!'

'That's silly!' said Jane, hugging the puppy. 'And what I'd like to know is, what your mother and father said when you brought a puppy home. Why didn't they find out whose it was?'

'Nobody knew,' said Sam. 'We looked after him ourselves. He's nice and clean now, and we gave him proper food and he was happy. And in any case,' said Sam, looking fierce, 'why didn't you two look after him properly? At least we didn't lose him!'

Jane and Paul didn't answer. Then Jane said, 'He looks all right. It's a good thing for you that he *is* all right! I think you're very naughty children, stealing our puppy.'

'We didn't steal him, we didn't!' said Rosie. 'We loved him!'

'At least *we* looked after him properly!' said Sam again, and Rosie began to cry miserably.

'Oh, come on, Rosie, let's go home,' said Sam, upset to hear his sister crying so loudly. 'The puppy's all right. And we enjoyed looking after him for a while.'

'You'd better let him come with us now,' said Paul.

Sam frowned as a thought came to him. 'How do we know *you're* the right owners? Our cousins said there's a notice in the post office window, but you might be *pretending* he belongs to you!'

'Don't be silly!' shouted Jane, upset.

But her brother said, 'Perhaps Sam is right. If we all go down to Mr Williams, then he or Miss Morgan will tell Sam and Rosie it's all right and that he *does* belong to us.'

'Why didn't you take him to Mr Williams before?' asked Jane, still angry.

Rosie hung her head. 'I'm sorry,' she said. 'It was my fault. We were going to, honestly we were. Only I just wanted one more night with dear little Star.'

Paul set off down the path and Jane followed, cuddling the puppy. Sam got onto his bike and Rosie began to push the empty pram

70

down the path. 'I really thought it was my wish come true,' she said. 'It's not fair! Now I've got used to a real, live, warm, cuddly puppy, I don't think I'll ever really enjoy playing with my dolls again. I want another puppy!'

'Oh, you'll soon love your dolls again,' said Sam, pedalling in front. 'And they'll be very glad to see you. I expect they've missed you a lot while you've been busy with the puppy.'

The four children walked in silence down the lane and soon got to Mr Williams at the veterinary surgery. He was in the drive and saw them coming. 'Oh!' he called. 'Wonderful! You've found your puppy!'

'Yes,' said Paul, smiling. 'These two,' and he turned round and pointed to Sam and Rosie, 'found him and looked after him for us.'

'Oh,' said Mr Williams, looking puzzled. 'Well, as long as he's back with you again, everything must be all right.' He had a quick look at the puppy, who barked 'He's very well,' said Mr Williams. 'He *has* been well looked after!'

Paul and Jane took the puppy and began to walk back to their house.

Rosie blew her nose.

Sam said, 'Come on, Rosie. We'd better get back or else Granny will be wondering where we are.'

When they got near to their home, Sam looked at Rosie. Her eyes were very red and her face was streaked with tears. What on earth was Granny going to say if she saw her looking like that? She would soon find out about the puppy and how they had hidden him and looked after him. She might be very cross indeed.

They went to the playroom, but just as they got there Mrs Mills came flying down the path to them. 'Children, come up to the house quickly! Your mother's back again, and she's got a lovely present for you both! Hurry!'

'Oh!' said Rosie in delight. 'Mummy's back! I'll tell her everything. She'll understand. Oh Sam, she'll make everything come all right, won't she? She always does.'

The children raced to the house and burst in through the garden door. They ran to the lounge and there was Mummy, beaming all over her face, with Granny nearby.

'Mummy!' shouted the children and flung themselves on her. Mummy hugged them and kissed them, and then looked at Rosie in great surprise.

'Why, Rosie darling, what on earth is the matter? You look as if you've been crying and crying! Have you hurt yourself? Tell me.'

'Oh, Mummy, we had a secret,' said Rosie, tears coming into her eyes again. 'And the secret's gone, and I feel so unhappy.'

'Tell me all about it,' said Mummy. 'I'll make everything right for you. Just tell me.'

12

Everything comes right

Sam and Rosie poured out their secret and Mummy and Granny listened in amazement.

'We went for a walk with Big Belinda in the pram,' began Rosie, 'and while we went to get some honeysuckle something happened. Sam found a puppy in the bushes.'

'And we thought that Rosie's wish had come true and that we'd got a real live creature to look after,' said Sam. 'So we took the puppy home and kept him in the playroom for days and days.'

'*Kept* him!' said Granny, astonished. 'KEPT him! And I didn't know! How could you look after a puppy, you two, and feed him and everything?'

'Well, we did,' said Rosie. 'We bought some

tins of puppy meat, a bowl and some puppy biscuits, and cereal and milk. We fed him and bathed him, and I washed the pram sheets, just like I do for my dolls. He was a very happy puppy and we loved him.'

'And then today, when we took him out in the pram, two big children came up and told us off. They were very upset because we'd taken their puppy!' said Sam. 'They'd let him wander off at the swings and didn't realize until too late.'

'Oh, how awful,' said Mummy, amazed and alarmed at the same time. 'What a terrible thing to happen! Oh, children, fancy taking a real live puppy home with you. Surely, surely you couldn't look after him properly. Poor little thing!'

'He was a *happy* little thing,' said Rosie. 'Oh, Mummy, you can't imagine how nice it was to feel a warm, soft, cuddly puppy, and to have one that lapped up milk, and splashed in the bath and whimpered and barked and played football in the playroom with his nose!'

'And now poor Rosie is really unhappy because the puppy's gone back to his real owners,' said Sam.

'I think I'll always be unhappy now,' said Rosie, beginning to cry again. 'I shall miss the puppy so much.'

'No you won't,' said Mummy. 'I promise you, you won't. I'll put things right for you, quite, quite right. I'll make you happy again in one minute!'

The children stared at her. 'How, Mummy?' asked Sam, puzzled.

Mummy turned them round and pointed to the corner of the lounge. On the floor was the big Moses basket that she used to carry them in when they were babies. 'Go and look in the basket,' said Mummy.

The children went over to it. Someone was in the basket. Someone's fair, curly hair lay on the pillow. Two blue eyes, exactly like theirs, stared up at them.

'MUMMY!' cried Rosie, clasping her hands in joy. 'Mummy! It's a baby! Whose is it?'

'Mine, of course,' said Mummy. 'And Daddy's. And yours – she's your little sister. I've brought her back for you. She's the present I promised you. Do you like her?'

'No, I don't like her! I *love* her and *love*

her!' said Rosie, wild with delight. 'Can I hold her? Oh, look at her curly hair, and she's got blue eyes like you, Mummy. Mummy, she's beautiful! And she's ours.'

'She's much, much nicer than the puppy,' said Sam. 'I did like that puppy, but our baby is lovely, though she's so tiny, even tinier than the puppy!'

Mummy lifted the baby from the basket and put her into Rosie's arms. She held her gently. 'She's so soft and warm,' said Rosie. 'A hundred times better than a puppy or a doll. I shall always, always love her.'

'Families ought to love one another,' said Mummy. 'They belong together, don't they, Granny?'

Granny nodded. She had been so surprised at the story told by the children that she hadn't been able to say a word. But how glad she was that everything had come right for Rosie in the end.

'What a good thing those two children took their puppy back,' said Sam suddenly. 'We wouldn't have had time to look after him as well. And we couldn't have helped loving our baby the most. Mummy, you came home at exactly the right minute.'

'Can I bath her? And feed her? And help with her washing and ironing?' asked Rosie. 'You're not going to have a nanny for her, are you, Mummy?'

'No. You're so good with your dolls, I thought you could help me with her,' said Mummy. 'And now that I know you've looked after a real puppy for so long, well of course you can help with our own baby.'

Rosie was very happy. She sat nursing her baby sister, her eyes still red from crying, but a happy smile on her face, and a feeling inside that everything, everything was quite all right again now.

'I've got another sister,' said Sam. 'I always wanted another sister. I shall teach her how to play cricket, and run fast, and I'll lend her my new football. It will be nice to have a baby sister. And I shall always like *you* as well, Rosie!'

Just then the phone rang and Granny went to answer it. When she came back she beamed at the two children. 'That was Paul,' she said. 'He and Jane have forgiven you for taking their puppy. Their mother says it was their fault anyway for being so careless as to lose him. They've invited you round next Saturday afternoon, so you can play with the puppy and have tea with them. And,' said Granny, 'they've decided to call him Star as well!'

'Oh,' said Rosie and she clapped her hands. 'Yes, I'd like to go and see Star. But really our new baby's so much more exciting now!'

Everyone laughed.

'How you kept your secret I don't know,' said Granny. 'I really, really don't! What an amazing pair of children you are, and what a very strange secret!'

It was, wasn't it? But everything came right in the end. You should see their baby now! She's exactly right for Rosie's pram, so sometimes Mummy lets her wheel the baby round the garden in that one, instead of her own baby buggy. There goes Rosie, as proud as any big sister could be. Goodbye Rosie. Goodbye Sam. It *was* nice to share your secret with you!

Other titles in the 'Fabulous Four' series:

Four in a Family

John and Sarah's Dad is in hospital, and they'd love to take him some presents. The only problem is that they don't have any money!

Together with their cousins, Sam and Rosie, they begin to make plans. The Fabulous Four are full of ideas about how they can earn some money, but will they really manage it? And what is Rosie's big secret for earning the most?

The Birthday Kitten

Sam and Rosie's birthdays are coming up soon, and what they've always wanted is a puppy or a kitten. But their Mum wants them to wait.

Before their big birthday party, Sam and Rosie go down to the pond to play with Sam's new sailing boat. While there, they hear a splash and see a bag in the water with something moving in it. To their surprise, they discover a tiny kitten, shivering and very hungry.

Can they keep him without Mummy and Daddy knowing? How will they nurse him back to life? And who would want to throw him in the pond?

The Hidey Hole

It's blackberry picking time, and Sam, Rosie and John go out to the common. But when they get there, they see that all of the bushes have already been picked. Then they discover a better place to go blackberrying – the neighbour's garden! And to their surprise, they find an amazing hidey hole there.

What do they find inside it? And who has been using it as a secret place?

The Four Cousins

The Fabulous Four learn about some needy children in Africa and decide to help. They all start doing jobs to earn money, but Sarah and John soon turn to reading or snoozing instead of working hard. But when they hear how much money Sam and Rosie have saved up, they try to earn their own share.

How much will the four cousins earn? And what will be their wonderful reward?